Newca

Newcas

MISCHIEF

Pesky Monkeys

Other titles in the Mo's Mischief series:

Four Troublemakers
Teacher's Pet
Pesky Monkeys
You're No Fun, Mum!

MO'S MISCHIEF

Pesky Monkeys

Hongying Yang

HarperCollins *Children's Books*

First published in China by Jieli Publishing House 2003
First published in Great Britain by HarperCollins *Children's Books* 2008
HarperCollins *Children's Books* is a division of HarperCollins*Publishers* Ltd
77-85 Fulham Palace Road, Hammersmith, London W6 8JB

The HarperCollins *Children's Books* website address is
www.harpercollinschildrensbooks.co.uk

1

Text copyright © Hongying Yang 2003
English translation © HarperCollins Publishers 2008

Illustrations © Pencil Tip Culture & Art Co 2003

Hongying Yang asserts the moral right to be identified
as the author of this work

ISBN-13 978-0-00-727341-6
ISBN-10 0-00-727341-X

Printed and bound in England by
Clays Ltd, St Ives plc

THE BIG BLACK CAT
AND
THE BIG WHITE CAT

Mo Shen Ma was on his way to Grandma and Grandpa's house for the summer holidays. Mo's grandparents lived at the foot of a big mountain in the countryside that was also a Nature Reserve. Loads of rare and protected species lived on the mountain. Grandma always shut the garden gate as soon as it got dark. She said there were wild tigers on the mountain that liked to carry away small children in their mouths and eat them in their mountain lairs.

Mo thought Grandma was only trying to frighten him, because he'd never seen a wild tiger, and he had explored all around Grandma and Grandpa's house, whenever he went there to visit.

As soon as Mo's dad's car stopped, an old white goose came over, swaying from side to side, and honking as if to greet them.

When Mo and his dad got out of the car, they heard someone shouting, "We have guests!" But Mo didn't recognise the voice. Who was it?

Grandpa and Grandma hurried out to greet them.

"Guests?!" Grandma said, looking up. "This is my son and my grandson. They're not guests! They're family!"

Mo looked up too, wondering who Grandma was talking to. There was a birdcage hung in the porch of the house, and in it was a brown, yellow-beaked bird.

"That's Grackle," said Grandma. "He always speaks when he sees people. Don't you, Grackle? He's *much* better than a parrot."

"Thank you! Thank you!" said Grackle, nodding vigorously.

They went into the garden. Mo's dad sat and talked for a while then drove away. He had to go back to work in the city.

After Mo's dad had left, the old white goose came into the garden, swaying and honking.

"Go!" Grandpa patted the old white goose on its head. "Some guard-goose you are. Go and guard the gate! What are you following us for?"

Mo thought this was strange. "Grandma," he said. "Didn't you used to have a big yellow guard dog? Why don't you let the dog guard the gate, instead of the goose?"

"Good question," said Grandpa. "Where's the dog, Grandma?"

"It's sleeping. It's tired out from catching mice last night!"

What kind of a dog catches mice? thought Mo. Cats were supposed to catch mice, not dogs! So what was the cat up to? Mo was sure there had been a big black cat last time he'd visited.

"Where's the big black cat, Grandma?" he asked.

"The big black cat? Ah! It's a very sad story, Little Jumper."

"Did it die?"

"I would feel happier if it had died," Grandma sighed. "But it's up in the tree."

"Well that's all right then!" said Mo. "Cats like playing in trees."

His Grandma looked at him. "Well, Little Jumper, this one has been in the tree for three months, come rain or hard weather."

"It must be starving," said Mo.

"We send it three meals a day," said Grandpa. "Actually, I'm just about to take its dinner along. Would you like to come with me?" Mo nodded enthusiastically. Grandpa put a bowl of pork and rice and a long rope in a basket, then they walked to the tree, which was at the far end of the garden. Grandma and Grandpa's garden was so big that it was a five minute walk to the tree.

Mo looked up and saw the big black cat. It was lying on a branch, staring at a spot behind Mo and Grandpa, a distressed expression on its face.

"Come down and eat your meal, big black cat!" shouted Mo.

"It won't come down! We have to send the meal up to it," said Grandpa.

Mo looked up at the tree. It was very tall. And even

though he could jump very high, Mo didn't think he could reach the cat. How was Grandpa going to get the food up there?

Grandpa took the long rope out of the basket, tied one end of it to the handle of the basket, then threw the other end up into the tree. The rope was now looped over the branch next to the cat.

As Grandpa pulled on the rope, the basket lifted into the air, closer and closer to the cat. The big black cat jumped gently into the basket, and Mo heard small slurping noises as it ate its food.

After a while, the big black cat jumped out of the basket and lay down on the branch again, staring at the same place, with an even more distressed expression than before.

"Why does the big black cat stare like that, Grandpa?"

Grandpa turned and pointed at the house opposite. "The big black cat likes the big white cat that lives over there. But the big white cat's owner doesn't like our cat, so he keeps the big white cat tied up at home. And our cat misses the big white cat so much that it climbed up into this tree, so that it could look at the white cat every day. From up there, it can see through the window."

"And it won't ever come down?"

"We've tried everything," Grandpa said. "Once there was a storm that lasted a day and a night. The big black cat was shivering with cold, but he still wouldn't come down."

What a stubborn cat! But Mo was stubborn too, and he was sure he could get the cat down if he tried.

"Come on, let's go home," Grandpa said. "We need to take Hurricane Hog back for his dinner."

"Who's Hurricane Hog?"

"He's our pig."

"Why is he called *Hurricane* Hog?"

"Because he runs like the wind."

A pig that can run like the wind? Mo wanted to see that at once! "Let's go and find him!" he said.

"You can't find him. He never lets people know where he is."

"Then how do you get him, to give him his dinner?"

Grandpa laughed. "I have my ways."

When they got home, Grandpa took out a horn and began to blow it, standing at the garden gate. Though Grandpa blew the horn for a long time, the pig was nowhere to be seen.

"Let's go in and wait. He'll come."

Just as he went into the house, Mo saw the old white goose standing at the garden gate, flapping its wings angrily.

"Hurricane Hog," said Grandma with a smile. "The old white goose always does that when she sees him coming."

And then, like a hurricane, the pig rushed through the door!

Mo looked at the pig: it had a very small belly but a pair of very large eyes. And it had very special ears. Usually, pigs had floppy ears. But this pig's ears stood up straight.

Mo pressed the pig's ears down. Straightaway, they bounced back up. He tried again. They bounced back again. The pig grunted, then nuzzled Mo!

"He likes you, Little Jumper," smiled Grandma.

Mo thought Grandpa and Grandma's animals were very strange: a cat who lives in a tree, a dog who likes catching mice, a goose who guards the gate, and a pig who runs like the wind – whatever next?!

★

Mo took over feeding the cat from Grandpa. He wanted to work out a way to get the cat down from the tree, and bring it home.

Mo also learned how to make cat meals: cutting spiced pork liver into pieces and then mixing them with rice. Today he placed the meal in the basket and headed for the tree. He tied one end of the rope to the handle of the basket, then threw the other end into the tree, as his Grandpa had done. Mo pulled the rope and the basket lifted up.

When the big black cat smelled the meal, he jumped into the basket.

Mo suddenly let go of the rope. The basket began to drop, clattering down the tree trunk.

Just before the basket hit the ground, the big black cat jumped out and gripped on to the trunk of the tree. Then it climbed back up to its branch.

Mo giggled.

The cat hissed at him.

★

The next time Mo delivered the basket to the cat, it turned its head to one side and ignored him. It wasn't going to be fooled again.

"Fine!" said Mo. He pulled the basket down again. "Starve yourself. See if I care."

Mo carried the meal back to Grandma's. Grackle, who was standing on the roof, cried joyfully, "Mo is back! Mo is back!"

Grandma looked in the basket. "Why didn't the cat eat its meal?" she asked Mo. "Did you make it angry?"

"It didn't eat this meal, but it *will* eat the next one."

"Oho!" said Grandma. "Little Jumper, you don't know that cat! It has a temper like you wouldn't believe! It's more stubborn than a billy-goat."

And Grandma was right! Mo sent the cat meals after meal, but it refused to eat them all.

Two days went by. The big black cat ate nothing, crouching on the branch of the tree. It looked ill.

"Eat some food, please!" Mo pleaded.

The big black cat closed its eyes, pretending not to hear.

"You'll starve to death if you don't eat, you silly big black cat."

The big black cat opened its eyes but didn't move. It was determined not to be fooled by Mo again.

"I'll go and get a fish for you!"

Mo went home, fetched his Grandpa's fishing rod and then ran to the vegetable plot. He dug up some earthworms as fish bait. Then he went to the pond and quickly caught a small fish.

Mo ran back to the tree with the fish flapping in his hand.

"I'm back with a fish, big black cat!"

The big black cat didn't even blink.

Mo lifted the fish on the rope. The small fish flipped near the cat's face, but the cat ignored it.

"Big black cat! Come on! Eat the fish!" Mo shouted.

Just then, a boy ran out of the house opposite the

tree. He was about Mo's age.

"What's all the racket?" the boy asked.

"The big black cat is starving itself to death. And it's all my fault," cried Mo.

"No. It's not your fault. It misses my white cat. That's why it's sad."

Mo looked at the boy. He had big round eyes and hairy ears like a bat.

"I'm Bat Ears," said the boy.

"I'm Mo Shen Ma," said Mo, "but my family call me Little Jumper because when I was a baby I used to jump very high!"

Bat Ears had watched Mo sending the meals up to the cat three times a day. He wanted to make friends with this boy from the city, but his mum and dad wouldn't let him because Mo was part of the family with the big black cat. Bat Ears' parents *hated* the big black cat.

"I don't want the big black cat to die, Bat Ears," said Mo.

Bat Ears looked up at the cat. "I don't want it to die, either," he said.

Suddenly, Mo had an idea! "Bat Ears, you said just now that the big black cat misses your big white cat.

16

So why don't you go and let the big white cat out?"

"Oh, I wouldn't dare," said Bat Ears. "Mum and Dad would be cross with me."

"Then don't tell them! Let it out secretly!"

"I'll try," said Bat Ears, looking nervous.

Bat Ears ran back to his house and went in. Soon enough, he came back out again, followed by the big white cat. The big white cat saw the big black cat in the tree and began to cry.

"Meow, meow, meow."

The big black cat in the tree meowed back.

"Take the cat back inside, at once!" someone shouted. Mo and Bat Ears turned to see a man standing outside his house. It was Bat Ears' dad. He was a little man with a round face and red cheeks. He looked *very* angry.

So the white cat went back inside, and the black cat stayed in the tree, looking very sad indeed. It wailed like a baby, and soon other villagers came to see what all the fuss was about.

"Ah!" they said. "Poor big black cat! It's missing the big white cat."

Mo didn't understand why Bat Ears' parents wouldn't let the big white cat and big white cat be together. He decided to ask his grandparents.

"Why are Bat Ears' parents so mean?" he asked. "What did the big black cat ever do to them? Why do they hate it so much?"

"You're too young to understand," said Grandma.

But the more they refused to tell, the more Mo wanted to know.

Mo went to find Bat Ears. He took some chocolate, to tell Bat Ears he was sorry about getting him shouted at by his dad.

"Why do your parents hate the big black cat, Bat Ears?"

Bat Ears was only interested in the chocolate. He didn't seem to hear Mo.

"I'm talking to you, Bat Ears!"

"Mmmm, yummy – SO delicious!"

Mo was cross. "I'm asking you about the big white cat and the big black cat!"

Bat Ears put out his tongue, licked off all the chocolate around his mouth, and then said, "The big black cat likes the big white cat. The big white cat likes the big black cat too. But my mum and dad won't let them be together."

"Why?"

Bat Ears closed his eyes and shook his head, and Mo had to give him another piece of chocolate before he would explain. "If the big black cat and the big white cat were allowed to be together, then the big white cat would have black-and-white kittens."

Mo didn't understand. Even if the big white cat had black-and-white kittens, there was nothing wrong with that! Female cats always had kittens!

Bat Ears said, "My mum and dad say that pure-bred white cats are valuable, and pure-bred black cats are valuable, but black-and-white cats are not. So they've tied the big white cat up. The big black cat had to climb up that tree, because it was the only way he could *see* the big white cat."

Mo gave Bat Ears another piece of chocolate. "Well, I'm going to get the big black cat and the big white cat back together – will you help?"

"How?"

Mo whispered a plan to Bat Ears. Bat Ears didn't like it because he thought it would get him into trouble. But when Mo asked him to give back the chocolate he had eaten, Bat Ears had to agree – he knew it was *impossible* to return chocolate that had already been eaten.

Mo went back to his grandparents' house and took his suitcase out from under the bed. The case was filled with his favourite food: crystal jellies made of fresh fruit, almond-chocolate pies, lemon rice crackers, strawberry lollipops, orange and pineapple sweets... These things were common in the city, but not here, in a mountain village.

Mo put all the sweets into a big rucksack and took the bag over to Bat Ears' house.

Without a word, Mo took the sweets out one by one. Soon the table was piled with sweets of all colours.

"Wow, look at all those sweets!" Bat Ears rushed at the table, but his dad suddenly came through the door and grabbed him by the elbow. Bat Ears cried out. "I want to have them! Let me eat them!"

Bat Ears' dad ignored his son, and turned instead to Mo, looking at him suspiciously. "Why are you giving us all these sweets for no reason?"

"I'm begging you to save the big black cat. It's dying in the tree."

"I'm not a cat doctor, how can I save it?"

"Set your big white cat free and then the big black cat will come down from the tree."

"What nonsense, you silly boy!" Bat Ears' dad shouted. "Now go home to your Grandma's house!" He put the sweets back into the bag, shoved it into Mo's hands, and pushed him towards the door.

Bat Ears began to cry very loudly. "WAA WAAA WAAAA!"

Mo couldn't help laughing as he walked out of Bat Ears' home. The plan was going to work. Bat Ears was such a good actor!

At dinnertime, Bat Ears' mother came to find Mo. She was looking worried.

"Bat Ears is on a hunger strike. He didn't eat his lunch, and now he won't eat his dinner."

Mo remembered what Bat Ears' dad had said. "I'm not a *boy* doctor. How can I help?"

"You brought us lots of sweets earlier, didn't you?"

"Yes, I did. But your husband threw me out."

"I'm very sorry, Mo Shen Ma, he shouldn't have done that." Bat Ears' mum smiled. "Our Bat Ears had never seen so many sweets in his life, and now he's upset that they're gone! He said if he wasn't allowed any sweets, he would never, ever eat again!"

Bat Ears really was a *brilliant* actor! Mo was happy. He knew the plan was working! But he was careful not to show it to Bat Ears' mum. "I'll give you the sweets," he said. "But not for free."

Bat Ears' mum took out a wad of notes. "I'll pay!"

"I don't want money," Mo said, craftily. "I just want you to set the big white cat free, so that the big black cat will come down from the tree."

Bat Ears' mum sighed. "OK, you win."

Bat Ears' was allowed to release the big white cat that evening. It climbed up the tree, and curled up next to the big black cat. They both purred very loudly.

THE FISH TREE

The big white cat didn't get down after it climbed up the tree. It stayed beside the big black cat and each one wailed, one after the other.

The big black cat raised its head from time to time, then slumped down again. It didn't have the strength to raise its head!

"It's because the big black cat is hungry." Bat Ears said. "Let's get some fish for the big black cat, Little Jumper. All cats love fish!"

"It's dark. Where will we get fish from?"

"We've got a new fish pond down the hill. You wait

here. I'll go home and get something to catch fish with."

★

After a while, Bat Ears came back to the tree, holding a fishing net in one hand and a tin can in the other.

Mo looked inside the can.

"It's fish food," said Bat Ears.

"But it's so late. The fish will all be asleep. Will they eat the fish food?" said Mo .

"Fish don't close their eyes even when they sleep," said Bat Ears. "And they're greedy! They'll come when they see fish food spreading on the water."

When they got to the fish pond, Bat Ears carefully put the fishing net down into the water and then scattered some fish food on the water above the net.

Suddenly, the quiet surface of the water bubbled up. Mo thought a monster was about to jump out! In the moonlight, Mo could see flashes of sparkling silver and gold.

"Quickly, pull the net up!" he whispered to Bat Ears.

Bat Ears pulled up the net. Mo saw hundreds of tiny little fish.

24

Bat Ears told Mo that the fish were small, because it was a new pond.

Bat Ears and Mo got some twine, and threaded some fish together. Then they walked back to the tree, carrying their strings of little fish. They put them back in the fishing net, and lifted it as high as they could up into the tree, to tempt the big black cat and the big white cat with the smell of fresh fish.

But the big black cat was still on high alert. He was not going to be fooled by Mo again.

Mo was worried: "What can we do? The big black cat will starve to death if it won't eat."

"Maybe the big black cat would rather starve to death than eat something while we are here. He thinks we will trick him. If we went away, he might eat."

Bat Ears talked sense. But then Mo had an idea!

"The big black cat *might* eat if we can hang the fish in the tree."

This meant the boys had to climb up the tree. Bat Ears was used to climbing trees and he clambered up like a monkey. Mo had never climbed a tree, but he wasn't going to let Bat Ears think he was afraid! He watched where Bat Ears put his hands and feet, and followed him up.

 25

The big white cat thought the boys were trying to catch her, so she started to play hide-and-seek with them. The big black cat just looked sorrowful.

But Mo and Bat Ears' weren't trying to catch the cats, they had other things to do. They hung the fish over the branches and leaves of the tree. Silver and golden fish scales flashed in the moonlight.

Mo and Bat Ears climbed down the tree. They looked up at the masterpiece they had created, "It's so beautiful," Mo said. "It's as if the fish are growing out of the leaves."

Bat Ears suddenly felt scared. "Let's go," he said. "If my parents realise that the fish hanging in the tree are from our fish pond, they will never forgive me."

Bat Ears and Mo crept back home, as if nothing had happened.

★

The next day, several tourists came to the village. This was very unusual. Tourists usually went straight to the mountain, not to the village.

The tourists asked whoever they met: "Excuse me! Could you tell us where the fish tree is?"

"A fish tree?" The villagers laughed. "These silly city

people, do they really think fish grow in trees?"

"We were told by someone who had seen it. So here we are," said the tourists.

"There's no such tree here in our village," replied the puzzled villagers.

The tourists were disappointed. Then along came Mo...

"Young man, do *you* know where the fish tree is?" they asked.

"The fish tree?" Mo smiled sweetly. "Oh yes, I'm going there now. Follow me." Mo thought he might get a tip from the tourists, for showing them the way.

Mo led the tourists to the fish tree. They were all AMAZED when they saw it.

"I've never seen such a *beautiful* tree."

"How come the tree has grown fish?"

"Look! Look! There are two cats in the tree, too!"

Mo couldn't believe what he was seeing. The big black cat, who was so quiet and hungry yesterday, was now full of energy and was frolicking around the tree, eating fish.

"Wow!" said one of the tourists. "So that's what cats eat in the wild!"

"Yes," said Mo. "There are many fish trees in this

part of the world. And all of them are full of wild cats."
He couldn't tell the tourists that HE had put the fish in
the tree. Then Bat Ears' parents might find out, and
they'd both be in trouble for taking fish from the new
pond!

"Amazing," said a lady tourist, as she took a picture
of the big black cat. "I always wondered why cats like
the taste of fish so much, when all they seem to each
is mice."

"Ah," said Mo, wisely, "they only eat mice in the
city, because there are no fish trees around."

The woman nodded and smiled. "You must be
right!"

Mo beamed with pleasure.

After that, the tourists spread the story of the fish
tree so far and wide that soon many more tourists
came to the village to see it. And all because of Mo's
mischievous plan!

HURRICANE HOG

Mo knew that Grandma's animals were a little strange. Her big yellow dog liked to catch mice. And her big black cat lived in a tree. But the strangest animal of all was Hurricane Hog.

Every morning, Mo would hear a bang as Hurricane Hog burst through the gate of the pigsty. Soon afterwards, he would hear Grackle shouting: "Hurricane Hog is coming out! Hurricane Hog is coming!"

Hearing Grackle's shouting, the old white goose, who guarded the gate from early in the morning, flapped its wings and dodged aside in case Hurricane Hog knocked it down.

"Was Hurricane Hog born to run fast, Grandma?" Mo asked one day.

"Not exactly!" Grandma said. "Hurricane Hog was no different from the other piglets when he was born. But later, he didn't like being kept in the pigsty all day long, just eating and sleeping, so he started to go out early in the morning and come back in the evening."

"But where does he go?" asked Mo.

"I don't know, Little Jumper," Grandma shook her head. "He runs faster than the wind, and is soon out of sight. What does it matter where he goes?"

But Mo was not satisfied. He wanted to know where Hurricane Hog went and what he did all day long.

He decided to track the pig.

The next morning, Mo was waiting at the gate when Grackle shouted "Hurricane Hog is coming!"

Out rushed Hurricane Hog!

Mo started to run after the pig. But after a while they came to a river. Hurricane Hog jumped over the river, but it was too wide for Mo, so he had to go over the bridge. By the time he got to the other side of the river, Hurricane Hog had disappeared.

Mo was annoyed. He had to walk back to the village and he still didn't know where the pig went all day. Then he met Bat Ears riding his bike.

Bat Ears laughed when he heard that Mo had tried to track Hurricane Hog.

"You couldn't track that pig, even if you were on horseback!" he said.

Mo was puzzled: "But how can a pig run faster than a horse?"

"Because he goes training!" Bat Ears pointed at a mountain in the distance, "You see that mountain? You see that winding mountain road?"

Mo saw the winding mountain road. It was like a white band on the green mountain, winding all the way to the peak.

"Every morning, Hurricane Hog runs all the way up that road to the top of the mountain," explained Bat Ears. "And then he runs all the way down again."

So that's what Hurricane Hog got up to all day! Mo laughed. "But why does he do it?"

Bat Ears scratched his head and narrowed one of his eyes: "Maybe the pig wants to be a horse?"

Mo had an idea. "If Hurricane Hog *wants* to be a

horse, we can help him. We'll ride him! Let's try when he comes back tonight!"

When the sun had gone down Mo and Bat Ears heard Grackle shouting, "Hurricane Hog is coming! Hurricane Hog is coming!"

Mo and Bat Ears put their plan into action. They carried a bucket of pigswill out to the yard.

Although Hurricane Hog was an unusual pig, he still ate like a pig. His appetite was HUGE and he made lots of slurping noises when he ate. He was so busy eating that he didn't realise Bat Ears had put a saddle on his back and a rein around his neck.

Hurricane Hog had finished his supper – he looked very content.

He let Bat Ears lead him out of his pen, with the rein.

Bat Ears carefully climbed on to Hurricane Hog's back. He pulled on the rein and, at the same time, gently clipped the pig's tummy with his legs. On hearing Bat Ears shout "Go!", Hurricane Hog started to run.

Hurricane Hog ran just like a horse!

Bat Ears rode the pig for a lap, then asked Mo to have a go.

"Don't be scared, it was your idea!" he said. "It's just like riding a horse."

Mo knew how to ride. He had been horse riding lots of times with his dad. But riding a horse was different to riding a pig…

"Go!" shouted Bat Ears, when Mo had settled on the pig's back.

Hurricane Hog started to run as soon as Mo pulled the rein and clipped its tummy.

Hurricane Hog was fast! The wind whistled past Mo's ears and houses flashed by in front of his eyes. But quite soon Mo's bottom was feeling a bit sore, and his legs were aching, so he rode the pig back to the garden.

Then Mo had another idea. "Bat Ears, do you think Hurricane Hog can pull a cart?"

"We don't have a cart in my house," said Bat Ears.

"Grandma has one. Let's drag it out. Hurricane Hog can pull the cart with us in it."

Mo and Bat Ears dragged the cart out quietly. They put straps under the pig's tummy to make sure he could pull it without getting his legs tangled up. Bat Ears grabbed the reins, and Mo sat on the cart.

"Go, pig, Go!" they shouted.

Unbelievably, Hurricane Hog pulled the cart with the boys on it.

"Hurricane Hog is too clever to be just a pig," laughed Mo.

"Then what is he?" asked Bat Ears.

"He's a SUPERPIG! He flies like the wind and he's so smart! He's the cleverest animal in the whole world."

SKATEBOARD AND ROLLER SKATES

Now Mo had proved that Hurricane Hog was very clever, he decided to see what else the pig could do. He'd brought his skateboard with him to Grandma's. Would Hurrican Hog be able to ride it?

Bat Ears had never been on a skateboard before.

"It looks easy, almost the same as roller-skating," said Bat Ears.

Bat Ears jumped on to the skateboard. The board slipped from under his feet and he fell flat on his bum.

"I'm not trying again," said Bat Ears. Roller-skating is *much* easier." He went home to get his roller-skates.

"You have a try then, Hurricane Hog! You're such a clever pig, you'll be able to do it straight away."

Mo put the pig's two front feet on to the skateboard. Even before Mo had shouted "GO!", Hurricane Hog had started running with his back feet, forcing the skateboard forward.

"Hurricane Hog!" Mo shouted. "Hurricane Hog, come BACK!"

But Hurricane Hog couldn't stop. When the skateboard had gained speed, the pig put his back feet on it and off he went.

Unbelievable! Hurricane Hog had learned to be a horse, to pull a cart and now to skateboard. He really was a brilliant superpig!

Mo was a little bit ashamed that a pig had become a better skateboarder than him in less than half an hour. But it had been *his* idea and that made him feel a bit better.

Bat Ears came back on his roller skates.

"Bat Ears, you've been beaten by a pig!" laughed Mo. "Hurricane Hog has already learned to skateboard."

"But he doesn't know how to roller skate," replied Bat Ears.

"Let's try him," said Mo, mischievously.

Mo was convinced there was nothing Hurricane Hog couldn't do – he was the cleverest animal in the whole world.

"Look! Bat Ears!" Mo pointed at a black dot in the distance, "Hurricane Hog is coming back!"

Hurricane Hog stood steadily on the skateboard, moving up and down along the slopes, sometimes turning left and sometimes right as if he was surfing. Mo had never seen anyone skateboard so well.

When Hurricane Hog came near, the two boys quickly jumped out of the way to avoid being knocked over. But to their surprise, Hurricane Hog even knew how to slow down and he stopped in front of them, grunting noisily.

"Hurricane Hog, stop skateboarding, and try roller-skating."

Bat Ears tugged at Mo and said, "But he doesn't have any roller skates."

"Well, you've got a pair, haven't you?" Mo pointed at the roller skates Bat Ears was wearing, "Take them off and put them on Hurricane Hog's hoofs."

"But he has *four* feet, and I only have one pair of roller skates," said Bat Ears patiently.

"I have a pair too," said Mo. "I'll go and get them, then we'll see if Hurricane hog can skate!"

A few minutes later, Mo came back with his roller skates.

The two boys struggled to put the roller skates on to Hurricane Hog's four feet.

As soon as they were on, Hurricane Hog started skating. INCREDIBLE! The boys jumped out of the way. That pig could move even faster on skates!

"Little Jumper, how *can* a pig be so clever?" wondered Bat Ears.

Mo thought carefully before answering. He thought about the dog who could catch mice, Grackle, the bird who could talk like a real person. The old white goose who guarded the gate—

"Perhaps all animals are as clever as humans," he said.

Then he had another idea!

Mo decided to see if the old white goose could skateboard.

The old white goose was not quite as quick to learn as Hurricane Hog. But it watched Mo very carefully as he showed it how to skate.

Then Mo put one of the old white goose's feet on to the skateboard. It stood steadily thanks to its large claws. The skateboard started to move forwards. The old white goose put the other foot on the skateboard. Although it was not as fast as Hurricane Hog, it did manage to stay on.

"Little Jumper, let's put roller skates on the old white goose's feet and see if it can roller skate too." said Bat Ears.

But the old white goose was a little scared of the

roller skates. It stretched out its wings and stood there not daring to move.

"Go, old white goose! Go!" said Mo.

Mo patted the old white goose on its back and the it began to move forwards. Very gracefully, the old white goose stretched out its left leg and then the right. It was roller skating! Although the old white goose was not as fast as Hurricane Hog, it moved more easily. And, it could skate in many different ways, even in circles when it stretched out its neck, opened its wings and leaned its body to one side.

"I'm right, aren't I Bat Ears? Animals *really* are as clever as human beings."

It had been a long day, but Mo was happy. Another of his ideas had worked.

But Grandma wasn't quite so happy when she heard what Mo had been up to with her animals. Would he ever stop with his mischief?

PRECIOUS GRANDSON, PRECIOUS POT

Time went by really fast and Mo had already been at Grandma and Grandpa's for two whole weeks. He was having a lot of fun, especially playing with Bat Ears and all Grandma's animals.

Mo liked playing so much that he often forgot to go into the house to have his dinner. Then the whole of Grandma's family would have to look for him. It was *always* the big yellow dog who found him. It would tug the corner of Mo's tunic or trousers and pull him back home.

When the old white goose saw Mo returning, it would stick its neck out, flap its wings and start honking.

Grackle would stick his head out of his cage and shout, "Little Jumper, have soup! Little Jumper, have soup!"

The big yellow dog was so proud of finding Mo that she would sit in front of Grandma, wagging her tail for a reward. Then Grandma would give her a meaty bone.

"Little Jumper, I have made some soup with chops and soybeans for you. Have it before it gets cold!" said Grandma.

After several bowls of soup, Mo said to Grandma, "Grandma, your soup is delicious, much better than the soup in big city restaurants!"

Grandma smiled and looked at the big soup pot she was holding, "Aha, Little Jumper. I'm glad you like my soup so much. The reason I make delicious soup is because I make it in this precious pot. This pot is an heirloom handed down by my grandma's grandma. It is a very special pot, so it makes very special soup."

Mo looked closely at the pot. It looked like an ordinary pot to him, nothing special. *But why does it make such delicious soup?* he wondered. *Is it magic?*

Mo was already very full from all the soup, but he still wanted more. He could see there was still a little left in the pot. He lifted the pot, tipped it right up to his lips and slurped out the very last drop. But there must have been some oil around the outside of the pot and it was hard to hold. Suddenly, the pot slipped from his hands and slid over his head – now Mo's head was inside the pot!

"What a naughty boy you are, Little Jumper! Take the pot off right away!" scolded Grandma. "I'm getting fed up with your mischief-making."

Grandma thought Mo was just playing.

Mo *wanted* to get his head out of the pot! But the mouth of the pot was too narrow and he couldn't lift it past his chin.

"My head's stuck inside, Grandma!"

His voice echoed inside the pot.

Grandma tried to lift the pot from Mo's head, but she couldn't.

Grandpa was out that day, so he couldn't even try.

Grandma was so worried that she ran to the door and shouted. "Help! Please help my grandson! "

Bat Ears was the first to run into the house, followed by some adults. Seeing that Mo's head was stuck in the pot, they began to joke with him. "Little Jumper, you're so silly!"

They thought it was funny, but Mo Shen Ma did NOT. Only he knew how uncomfortable it was having his head stuck in a pot.

Bat Ears' dad thought he might be able to get it off. "If the boy's head got in the pot, it must come out." He rolled up his sleeves and gripped the pot with both hands. Using all his strength, he tried to lift the pot off Mo's head. But he lifted Mo up as well as the pot. The pot was very definitely stuck.

"Aeeeeei," cried Grandma. "My precious grandson! And my precious pot!"

No one knew whether she was more worried about her grandson or the pot.

"Why don't we break the pot to get his head out?" suggested one of the villagers.

"No way! No way!" Grandma said, wringing her hands. "The pot is our heirloom. Without the pot, I cannot make delicious soup!"

"But which is more important, your grandson or your pot?"

"They are *both* important!" said Grandma.

There was nothing that could be done and everyone left shaking their heads.

"We must ask Wizard Ho for help," said Grandma.

"What does Wizard Ho do?" mumbled Mo, through the pot.

"Wizard Ho does what a magician does," answered Grandma.

"Then what does a magician do?" Mo continued.

"Stop it, Little Jumper! You're driving me mad." moaned Grandma.

"Can Wizard Ho really get the pot off my head?"

"Wizard Ho is a man with magical powers! Ordinary people won't be able to take it off but Wizard Ho *will*. When you meet Wizard Ho, you must bow to him, because he's a very powerful man and we don't want to get on the wrong side of him."

Grandma held Mo by the hand and took him to Wizard Ho's house.

"Please save my grandson, Wizard Ho. His head is inside this pot."

"Do you want the pot or your grandson?" asked the wizard.

"I don't believe it. He just said the same thing as all the other people," muttered Grandma.

"Please help me, Wizard Ho! I want BOTH!" she replied.

"Well, I have an idea. But you will have to pay me for it," said Wizard Ho slyly.

Mo really wanted to see what the magician looked like. But with his head in the pot, he couldn't see anything.

Wizard Ho wanted five hundred yuan. It was a lot of money but Grandma finally decided to accept. Her precious grandson and her precious pot were worth much more than five hundred yuan, even though one of them was a scamp.

Grandma pushed Mo in front of Wizard Ho, who was sitting at his magic table. Mo knew he had to bow to the wizard. But with a pot on his head, Mo couldn't see where he was going. He took a big step forward,

and made a deep bow to Wizard Ho.

CRASH!

The pot hit the table and broke into pieces. Mo's head was finally out!

"Oh no!"

Grandma beat her chest, feeling upset about her pot.

"Oh no!"

Wizard Ho beat his chest too. He was upset because he wouldn't get his money.

"OW!" Mo rubbed his head. He was upset because it was sore.

★

When they got home, Grandpa was back.

Grandma began to cry. "My heirloom – my precious pot has broken!"

"That's pot wasn't your heirloom," Grandpa said. "I broke your heirloom months ago! But I bought a new one exactly the same, from the market in town. It cost me two yuan."

"What? The heirloom pot was already broken? Then why is the soup I make so delicious?" Grandma asked.

"Grandma, it's because you're the best cook in the

whole wide world," laughed Mo. "I told you so!"

"Little Jumper, you're a mischievous boy, but you *are* my most precious grandson," said Grandma.

THE MEDDLESOME DOG

Grandma's big yellow dog was having puppies, but even though her tummy was big, she still liked to run around catching mice. Grandpa and Grandma said the big yellow dog shouldn't be meddling in the cat's business. If the big yellow dog hadn't started catching mice, the big black cat would have been kept busy in the house and garden. Then it wouldn't have got so friendly with the big white cat. Now the big black cat never came home.

"Little Jumper," said Grandma. "I want you to watch over the big yellow dog and stop it chasing mice. It's having puppies."

Grandma promised Mo that he could have a puppy to take back with him after the summer holidays.

Mo didn't go out to play so often after that. He stayed at home and kept watch over the big yellow dog to stop it from chasing mice.

But one day, the big yellow dog slipped out into Grandma's vegetable plot, and saw a big mouse!

"Woof! Woof!" The big yellow dog began to bark excitedly.

"Little Jumper! Don't let the big yellow dog run about. It's having puppies soon!"

But the big yellow dog had gone by the time Mo got out of the courtyard.

Mo could see the big mouse running ahead of the big yellow dog. They both ran and ran. The big yellow dog was about to catch up with the mouse, but the mouse suddenly stopped and lay dead still. The big yellow dog copied it.

"Aha!" said Mo. "They are both too tired to run any further!"

When Mo ran over, he found the big yellow dog

had given birth to a litter of puppies. One, two, three, four puppies in all.

Next Mo went to see the big mouse. But it wasn't a mouse at all. Whatever was it? It was the size of a cat, and had a bushy tail like a squirrel's. Its fur was grey, like a mouse, but it most definitely wasn't a normal mouse. It was a monster mouse!

This monster mouse had also produced a litter, but only two.

"Woof Woof!"

The big yellow dog wanted to chase the monster mouse again, instead of taking care of its four puppies.

The monster mouse stood up and scampered away. A few steps later, it stopped and turned its head to look at its two little monster babies lying on the ground. It couldn't bear to abandon them. But the big yellow dog was near.

"Big yellow dog, don't be silly!" Mo caught hold of the dog, "That's not a mouse you're chasing. Stop it!"

Mo squatted down and looked at the two little things that hadn't yet opened their eyes. The big yellow dog stared at them for a while too. Then she started to

lick the two little monsters clean.

Mo ran over to take a look at the big yellow dog's puppies. Their eyes weren't open either, and they needed licking too.

"Come over and look after your own puppies, big yellow dog!" he shouted.

But the big yellow dog was stubborn: she wanted to look after the two little monster mice babies.

"Stop poking your nose into other animals' business," scolded Mo.

Mo took off his T-shirt and spread it on the ground. He carefully placed the four little puppies and the two little monsters on the T-shirt and wrapped them in it. He took all the babies and the big yellow dog home.

"Grandpa! Grandma!" Mo said when he entered the door, "The big yellow dog has had her puppies!"

Grandpa and Grandma came over to take a look: "One, two, three… Ah! The big yellow dog has had six puppies!"

"No. Two of them are not puppies."

Mo showed Grandpa and Grandma the two little monsters and told them what had happened. Grandpa and Grandma didn't know what these creatures were either.

"Quick, take the two little monsters outside and throw them away!" said Grandma to Grandpa.

Grandpa was about to take them, when—

"Grrrrrrrr! Grrrrrrr! Grrrrrrrr!"

The big yellow dog growled at Grandpa.

Grandpa had never seen the big yellow dog behave like this before. He was afraid he might be bitten. So he left the little monsters alone.

From that moment, the big yellow dog looked after the little monsters as its own babies. But it would not look after its own four little puppies.

The puppies were hungry, and cried.

Grandma was worried and got cross with the big yellow dog: "What a silly, meddlesome dog!"

Mo had an idea. He found some small plastic bottles and filled them with milk so that he could feed the puppies. Grandpa and Grandma came over and helped. They each fed one puppy but there was still one left unattended. Mo had another idea. He could teach the old white goose to feed the fourth puppy!

The old white goose was clever. It soon learned how to feed the puppy. Using its beak to clamp the small plastic bottle, it fed milk into the puppy's mouth.

The four puppies were growing day by day. So were the two little monsters fed by the big yellow dog.

Everyone in the village knew that another strange thing had happened at Grandma's house. People came to see the two little monsters. Then someone said the little monsters looked just like baby badgers.

Mo had an *Animal Encyclopaedia* in his bedroom. He looked up pictures of baby badgers in the book and compared them with the two little monsters. There was no doubt about it. The little monsters were definitely baby badgers.

Mo knew that badgers were wild animals, so the two little badgers had to be set free, so that they could return to their own mother. But how could he get to them since the big yellow dog kept such a close watch over them?

Grandma said, "We must take the two little badgers when the big yellow dog falls asleep."

"But that won't be possible," said Grandpa. "The big yellow dog always wakes up when it hears a mouse squeak, so it is bound to hear the baby badgers being taken."

Mo had another idea.

"We will have to make the big yellow dog extra sleepy," he said. "We will have to make him drunk on Grandpa's special spirits."

That night, Mo put some of Grandpa's special spirits in with the big yellow dog's water. The big yellow dog drank it all, and after a while, she started snoring loudly. She didn't even wake up when Mo prodded her.

Mo went to Bat Ears' house. The two boys carried a little badger each, and walked towards the thick mountain forest.

Next morning the big yellow dog woke up. When it found the two little badgers had gone, it started looking for them frantically.

"Woof! Woof! Woof!"

The big yellow dog was upset. The four little puppies were frightened and they crowded together, trembling. Mo felt a bit mean, and also a bit worried. If the big yellow dog knew that he had put the badgers back in the forest, she might not want to play with him any more.

The big yellow dog was sad for a long time, but she soon got fed up with grouching. She wandered out into the yard and her four little puppies followed her.

Then the big yellow dog turned round... and saw her own four little puppies. She had lost the baby badgers, but here were her own babies to look after.

And that's just what she did.

PESKY MONKEYS

Mo used to complain about time going by too slowly when he was at school in the city, but at Grandma's home in the countryside, it went too quickly. How he wished he could spend all day and all night playing!

One day, Mo was having lunch in the house, when he heard some frog calls. This was the secret sign he and Bat Ears used to contact each other. He put down his bowl and chopsticks and ran out of the house.

Grandma shouted at him, "Little Jumper, you haven't finished your lunch!"

But to Mo, having lunch was not as important as playing.

Bat Ears called out, "I saw a group of monkeys from the mountain stealing corn. Shall we go and look?"

"Yes, let's go!" agreed Mo, even though Grandma had told him to finish his lunch.

Bat Ears took Mo to a cornfield, where at least ten monkeys were breaking off corn cobs. There were corn cobs littered everywhere.

"Whose corn field is it?" asked Mo.

"It's Grandpa Hutu's." Bat Ears pointed at a small shack beside the cornfield. "That's him lying on the ground sleeping. The monkey sitting on a chair is the monkey king."

Mo looked. He saw an old man with a rosy glowing face lying beside the shack. He was fast sleep. On a chair nearby he saw a big, tall male monkey, with its legs crossed, looking as if he owned the place.

★

Bat Ears told Mo that there were several groups of monkeys in the Nature Reserve. Each group had its own monkey king and its own stomping ground.

Other groups of monkeys lived deep in the mountain, but this group liked getting up to mischief and annoying people.

Grandpa Hutu ate his lunch at noon every day. Then he would have a nap. The monkeys knew exactly when he went to sleep. When Grandpa Hutu was sleeping, the monkeys would come down the mountain and into the cornfield to mess up the corn. By the time Grandpa Hutu woke up in the afternoon, there were lots of tourists on the mountain, so the monkeys would go and meet them, blocking their way and robbing them. They liked cameras and rucksacks especially. The villagers called this group of monkeys the Pesky Monkeys. Their king was named Big Boss.

Mo and Bat Ears crept over to Grandpa Hutu. He was wearing a short white shirt that didn't meet his trousers. His stomach bulged out, like a big white football. Mo tickled Grandpa Hutu's stomach with a corn stalk. Grandpa Hutu slapped his tummy, then turned over and went back to sleep.

Big Boss heard the loud sound of a slap, and left the cornfield with his gang of monkeys.

Grandpa Hutu was still fast asleep... and snoring. Bat Ears told Mo that the monkeys would still act wildly and make trouble in the cornfield even if Grandpa Hutu was awake. The monkeys weren't scared of people one little bit.

Mo looked at Grandpa Hutu's fat stomach moving up and down. It was very funny. Then he had an idea! He whispered something to Bat Ears who fell about laughing. Then they both ran back home as fast as the wind.

Mo went to his room and picked up his paint and a paintbrush. He and Bat Ears ran back to Grandpa Hutu's cornfield. The old man was *still* asleep.

Mo looked at Grandpa Hutu's stomach carefully for a while. Then he used his paintbrush to paint two dark, thick eyebrows on Grandpa Hutu's stomach. Under the eyebrows he painted two eyes as big as apples. Around his tummy button, Mo drew a big, red, frightening mouth – a monster's mouth. Grandpa Hutu's tummy looked like a giant monster's face!

A——chooooooo!

Suddenly Grandpa Hutu did a huge sneeze, and got up. The giant's face on his stomach almost touched Mo's face. Mo was startled and he scampered off.

A——chooooooo!

On the second sneeze, Bat Ears scampered away too. The boys ran to a plot of bamboo forest and hid. But looking back at the cornfield, they saw that Grandpa Hutu had fallen asleep again!

After a while, the group of monkeys led by Big Boss returned to the cornfield. They picked the corn cobs – ripe and unripe – and littered them here, there and everywhere.

A——choooooooo!

Grandpa Hutu sneezed again. This sneeze was so loud it made the monkeys almost jump out of their skins. They blinked and looked around – they had no idea where the noise was coming from.

Then Grandpa Hutu woke up. He stood up and stretched.

The monkeys saw the face on Grandpa Hutu's tummy. Big Boss and his monkeys were so scared that they galloped desperately up the mountain.

Grandpa Hutu laughed. "Why are you running away? Are you scared of me?"

The Pesky Monkeys had never been frightened of

Grandpa Hutu before – he couldn't understand what had changed today.

Mo and Bat Ears giggled. Their plan had worked! They had taught those monkeys a lesson. But when they got back to the village, Bat Ears' mother told them that a group of monkeys had been misbehaving on the mountain. They'd thrown pine cones at a tourist, and even tried to steal her hat.

"It must be Big Boss and his gang," said Mo. "Let's go and ask Grandpa Hutu to frighten them off again."

"Ask Grandpa *Hutu* to deal with them?" Bat Ears' mum wondered. "But his corn field is always being damaged by the monkeys, and he hasn't been able to do anything about it."

Bat Ears' mum didn't know there was now a monster's face painted on Grandpa Hutu's stomach. A face that scared Big Boss and his monkey gang!

★

"Grandpa Hutu! Grandpa Hutu!" Bat Ears called Grandpa Hutu out from his cornfield, "The Pesky Monkeys have been annoying the tourists. Please go and, help them."

Grandpa Hutu just laughed. "What can I do to stop them?" he said.

Mo said in his *nicest* voice, "Apart from you, Grandpa Hutu, the monkeys fear nobody."

Remembering how the monkeys had run away from him a little while ago, Grandpa Hutu felt proud. "You're right, of course. Except for me, the monkeys fear nobody. Let's go!"

Mo and Bat Ears, followed by Grandpa Hutu, ran towards the mountain.

HOW TO SCARE MONKEYS

Scared out of their wits by the face on Grandpa Hutu's stomach, Big Boss and his Pesky Monkeys had fled back to the mountain.

There were many beautiful parts of the Nature Reserve but Pearl Beach was the most famous. There were waterfalls pouring down, their spray splashing out, like glittering pearls. That was why it was called Pearl Beach.

The tourists liked Pearl Beach. But so did the Pesky

Monkeys! They had forgotten about the monster's face as soon as they got there, and now they were being naughty again and getting up to all sorts of mischief.

Seeing the tourists posing for pictures, Big Boss came down from a tree, and walked behind one of them. Suddenly he pulled up her skirt.

The tourist squealed, and so did her friends.

The other monkeys in the trees thought it was very funny. Soon they had all jumped down from the trees and began to pull the tourists' clothes, and even grabbed their cameras and bags.

There was complete chaos at Pearl Beach.

Just at that moment, Grandpa Hutu, Mo and Bat Ears arrived.

"Stop that, you Pesky Monkeys!" shouted Grandpa Hutu.

He rushed at the monkeys with his stomach sticking out.

Big Boss saw the monster's face and ran away. All the other monkeys followed him.

"Thanks for helping us, grandpa!" smiled the tourists.

Grandpa Hutu now realised that it was the face painted on his stomach that had frightened the monkeys away. He pushed Mo in front of the tourists and said, "You should thank him! The face on my belly was his naughty work. He drew it when I was asleep. But it worked! When those monkeys came to make trouble in my cornfield, they were frightened by the face and ran away. So I can't be too cross with *this* young rascal!"

The tourists wanted to continue their trip on the mountain, but they were afraid of meeting the monkeys again. They asked Mo if he would draw scary faces on *their* clothes and T-shirts too. Then they would be safe...

★

... but it didn't last. Big Boss was a clever monkey and he soon realised that the painted faces were nothing to be afraid of. He and his band of monkeys were soon up to their old mischief again: they snatched cameras and bags and started playing football with them. They made faces at the tourists and then pulled on the tourists' T-shirts that had faces painted on them. The tourists were so fed up with the monkeys, they took off their T-shirts and ran down to the tourist shop to buy new ones.

Those naughty monkeys picked up the painted T-shirts and rushed down the mountain trying to scare the tourists on the road coming up!

Something had to be done about the Pesky Monkeys.

Mo was determined to come up with a new plan. He decided to ask his own Grandpa for advice.

"Monkeys are afraid of red lanterns." Grandpa said. "There used to be monkeys that ran into the village and did evil things. So each household hung a red lantern outside, and they didn't come any more."

Grandma said she would make red lanterns if Mo and Bat Ears would help her. They got some pieces of shiny bright red paper and thin bamboo strips, and made many red lanterns that night. Soon it was time to put this new plan into action.

★

The Pesky Monkeys usually went down the mountain twice a day, once at noon and once in the afternoon. Mo and Bat Ears let Hurricane Hog pull the flat cart with dozens of red lanterns on it, and went to the mountain *before* noon.

Bat Ears climbed up the trees at Pearl Beach as fast as a monkey, and hung the red lanterns in them. The bright red lanterns, set off by the green trees, looked extraordinarily beautiful.

In the middle of the day, when the sun was really bright, the Pesky Monkeys led by Big Boss went down the mountain. They saw the red lanterns in the trees when they came to Pearl Beach. They didn't act as wildly as usual and their eyes were full of fear. Even Big Boss looked afraid and he led the monkeys away.

"We did it! We did it!" yelled Bat Ears.

But Mo wasn't sure. He knew that the sly monkey king wasn't easily scared. He thought the monkeys would be back – and he was right! In the afternoon, those Pesky Monkeys, led by Big Boss, were back.

This time, the naughty monkeys didn't cower around Big Boss when they saw the red lanterns. Instead, they scattered in all directions, screeching and gibbering.

Mo and Bat Ears watched Big Boss climb up the tallest tree where the biggest red lantern was hung. With one swift swipe of his arm, he tore it down.

The smashed lantern drifted down to the ground.

Then all the other monkeys climbed up the trees, smashed the red lanterns and tore them down. In a very short time, all the red lanterns had fallen to the ground. And soon the Pesky Monkeys were up to their tricks again.

Mo was glum. "How cunning those monkeys are!"

After this plan failed, Grandpa came up with a new one: to set off firecrackers.

Grandpa said that once upon a time when the Spring Festival was coming, all the families in the village were making smoked bacon. The delicious smell had wafted up the mountain and attracted the Pesky Monkeys, who came down in the dead of night and stole all the bacon.

Over the next few days, monkeys kept coming to get bacon every day. But one day, two of the villagers were getting married. The monkeys came down to steal the bacon but were frightened away by the sound of firecrackers, which people in the countryside always set off during weddings. Since then, they had never come back for bacon again.

Bat Ears loved firecrackers and pestered his mum to buy some. Then he and Mo went to Pearl Beach with strings of firecrackers. They hung them in places they didn't think the monkeys would notice. Then they hid.

The Pesky Monkeys were on time. They rushed down to Pearl Beach as soon as the sun had moved right overhead. Mo wanted to catch them off their guard.

"Bat Ears, set the firecrackers off!" he whispered.

Crack, crack crack!

Crack, crack, crack, crack crack!

The noise was deafening, echoing around the mountain.

The Pesky Monkeys covered their ears. Big Boss was the first to come back to his senses. He realised that the ear-splitting sound of the firecrackers wasn't actually harmful. In fact, Big Boss did a break dance to the rhythm of the fireworks!

Mo was fed up. Big Boss had won this round too. But Mo was determined not to give up. He didn't believe in Grandpa's genius ideas any more – he had to come up with one of his own.

He thought hard. At first, the monkeys were scared of the monster's face on Grandpa Hutu's tummy. Next they were scared of the red lanterns in the trees. Then they were scared of the firecrackers... but none of those had scared them for long. What if Mo could combine all three ideas – surely that would scare the monkeys!

"Yes!" thought Mo, "that will work!"

That night, Mo and Bat Ears set to work with more red paper and paints. The next morning they got some more firecrackers and returned to the mountain.

Soon all the trees at Pearl Beach were hung with *scary-faced* lanterns. They looked like a Hallowe'en nightmare! Then Mo and Bat Ears hid. At noon, when the sun was shining brightly, the Pesky Monkeys came to Pearl Beach. They saw the new lanterns, they heard the firecrackers, but this time Bat Ears threw the firecrackers at the lanterns, so the sound seemed to come from them.

Crack crack crack! Crack-crack-crack!

Then Mo and Bat Ears started making ghostly noises:

"Whooo Whooo Whooo! Whooo Whooo Whoooo!"

The Pesky Monkeys were scared stiff. They screeched and ran wildly away into the mountain.

This time, they were really frightened. They ran all the way into the mountain caves and didn't come out for a very long time.

FAT MONKEYS
ON A DIET

Several days later, Bat Ears came to tell Mo that there was another group of monkeys coming to Pearl Beach. The king of this group of monkeys was called Old Yellow-Haired Ghost, but he and his monkeys were completely different from Big Boss and his gang. They never did bad things – they just liked having their photos taken with tourists.

Mo had never seen monkeys that liked having photos taken with people. So he went up the mountain with Bat Ears to have a look.

A dozen monkeys were having photos taken with tourists. And what posers they were! Some had their arms around tourists' shoulders; some were even sitting on their shoulders.

After taking photos, the tourists gave the monkeys food: pastries, chocolates and cans of drink; some even gave them fried chicken or roast duck.

The monkeys offered the best food to their monkey king, Old Yellow-Haired Ghost. With a chicken leg in one hand, and a can of cola in the other, Old Yellow-Haired Ghost looked like the most laid back monkey in the world. After finishing a can of cola, he took out another can, opened it skilfully and continued to drink. He had several bites of chicken leg, then dropped it aside and took a duck leg.

In a word, Old Yellow-Haired Ghost *never* stopped eating.

★

So it was no surprise that Old Yellow-Haired Ghost and all the monkeys in his gang were very fat. And they were only interested in fatty foods. They didn't want ordinary things like peanuts and fruit.

These monkeys were lazy. They did nothing except eat, sleep and pose for photographs, which made them fat... and slow.

Mo and Bat Ears were watching Old Yellow-Haired Ghost. He stood up with difficulty, clinging to a tree trunk. As he tried to walk he was gasping. With a thump, he fell over on the ground.

Mo and Bat Ears ran to Old Yellow-Haired Ghost.

"He's still alive!" Mo said, "Bat Ears, go and get help!"

The Wildlife Refuge office was not far from Pearl Beach. Bat Ears came back in a while with the warden and a vet.

The vet put on his stethoscope and listened to Old Yellow-Haired Ghost's heartbeat and then measured his blood pressure.

"What's wrong with it?" asked Mo.

"He's got Rich Man's Disease," the vet said. "He is suffering from obesity and high blood pressure. He has been eating people food and not monkey food."

The vet then examined several of the other fat monkeys, concluding that they were also suffering from Rich Man's Disease.

"They have to lose weight; otherwise they won't live long."

The warden was very worried. "Monkeys are animals," he said. "How can they lose weight when tourists keep giving them food?"

"Why not stop the tourists giving food to the monkeys?" asked Mo.

"No way," the warden shook his head. "The tourists like to feed the monkeys because then they can have photos taken with them. And if the tourists can't have photos taken with monkeys, they'll stop coming to the Nature Reserve. And if the tourists stop coming to the Nature Reserve, *then* where will we be?"

"I've got an idea," Mo said. He asked the vet, "What things can the monkeys eat which won't make them fat?"

"Coarse grain and fruit," said the vet.

"We can set up a small shop at Pearl Beach that only sells grain and fruit. If the tourists want to feed the monkeys, they can only feed them with the food bought from the shop rather than things they carry. That way, the monkeys get their food and the tourists get their photos!"

"That's a good idea," said the vet. "But the fat monkeys must also eat less. Put the coarse grain into *small* bags, and tell the tourists that they can only buy one small bag of grain or one piece of fruit to feed the monkeys. "

The warden said that he would go back and organise the monkeys' food.

★

There were many children in the village on their summer holidays. So when Mo and Bat Ears returned to the village and told them the news, the children were all willing to be in the FML – the Fat Monkey League. The children asked Bat Ears to be their captain. Bat Ears said that it was Mo's idea so he should be captain, and that he would be assistant captain.

Next day, all the members of the FML arrived at Pearl Beach early in the morning.

By the time the tourists had arrived at Pearl Beach, the fat monkeys had come down from the mountain. Old Yellow-Haired Ghost puffed as he walked among them.

The fat monkeys wanted something delicious to eat, so they went and had photos taken with tourists. Then they held out their hands to tourists asking for food.

At that moment the FML stepped in. They directed

tourists to the Monkey Food Store, and the tourists bought the small grain bags and pieces of fruit.

However, the monkeys were used to fatty food and they didn't seem to want to eat the grain and fruit at all!

Some members of the team were worried. "Captain Mo, the fat monkeys won't eat. Will they starve to death?"

"Of course not," Mo said confidently. "They *will* eat when they're hungry enough."

Old Yellow-Haired Ghost leaned against the big tree. He waited for a long time, but no monkey came

 to give him good things to eat. So he had to pick up a banana that had been dropped on the ground. He peeled the skin off, and began to eat it. He licked his

lips. That banana was good! Soon the other monkeys followed his example.

After a while, the monkeys were fed up with eating only small amounts of grain and fruit – they couldn't get full on that. So they had to climb the trees to pick wild fruit. That way, the monkeys became agile again, climbing up trees and leaping from branch to branch.

Another of Mo's plans had worked. What a summer he was having!

PROTECTED ANIMALS

Bat Ears hadn't come to play with Mo for two days. Mo thought perhaps he was ill and went to see him. Bat Ears was lying on his bed.

"Are you sick, Bat Ears?"

Mo put his hand on Bat Ears' forehead. It wasn't burning.

Bat Ears was sleeping soundly.

Mo pulled his ears. "Get up, Bat Ears," he yelled.

"Wha....a...t ?" Bat Ears did not open his eyes. "I haven't slept for two whole nights," he moaned.

What had Bat Ears been doing for two nights?

wondered Mo. More importantly, why hadn't he been included? Mo was determined to find out.

Mo pinched Bat Ears' nostrils to get him to wake up. But Bat Ears just opened his mouth, and breathed in and out through it.

Next, Mo blew in one of Bat Ears' ears. But Bat Ears stayed asleep.

Then Mo saw Bat Ears' bare feet sticking out of the duvet. He had an idea. He found a feather in the yard and went back into Bat Ears' bedroom. He started to tickle Bat Ears' feet with the feather.

"AAAAAAhhhhhhhhh, stop it, Little Jumper. My feet are *so* ticklish." squealed Bat Ears, now wide awake.

Mo said he would only stop if Bat Ears told him what he'd been up to.

Bat Ears held his finger to his lips as if to say to Mo, don't tell anyone I told you. "I went into the mountain with my dad," he whispered.

Mo wasn't happy. "Why didn't you ask me to go with you? We're best friends, aren't we?"

"My dad wouldn't let me."

"Why not?"

"My dad will be cross if I tell you."

"If you don't tell me, we're not going to be best friends any more," threatened Mo.

Bat Ears gave in. "We went to capture scaly anteaters in the mountains."

"But why?"

"Because their meat is good and their scales are used for medicine."

"Bat Ears, that's terrible!" Mo shouted. "Don't you know that scaly anteaters are pangolins, and pangolins are protected animals?"

Mo's teacher had taught the class about rare animals protected by the state. The pupils had to recite the names of these animals and they had a test about them. So Mo knew that pangolins were protected animals and no one was supposed to hunt them.

"Well, I didn't know that," said Bat Ears. "There are lots of pangolins in the mountains."

"It doesn't matter how many there are, Bat Ears, you're still not allowed to hunt them. Do you know what pangolins eat? They eat termites. And what do termites eat? Roots, trunks and anything made of wood, even house beams. If you capture all the pangolins, they won't be able to eat the termites, and then the termites will eat up all the trees on the mountain. Then when there are no more trees, thousands of termites will come down the mountain and eat the beams in your house. Then your house will crash down. Where will you live if that happens?"

Bat Ears was dumbstruck: "Is... is it that serious?"

"Do you think I'd joke about something like this?" replied Mo.

Bat Ears saw that Mo was deadly serious.

"Many people from the village go to the mountain to capture pangolins. Lixia went with his dad, so did Guyu, Daxue, Chungeng—"

"They were *all* committing crimes." Mo said quietly. "How many pangolins did you and your dad capture?"

"Maybe four or five," said Bat Ears.

"What?!" Mo screamed. He was horrified. "Four or five pangolins in one night. That's awful!"

Mo wanted to have a look at the pangolins Bat Ears had caught, but Bat Ears told him that his dad had sold them early this morning.

"Where did he sell them?"

"To a wild game restaurant. But I don't know which

one. There are so many and they're always full of tourists."

"Then we will look in every one, until we find those pangolins..."

RESTAURANT RIOT

The whole area around Mount Wanglong was a Nature Reserve. There were many wild game restaurants, large and small, near the entrance to the Reserve. Mo thought it was pretty silly that there were so many restaurants selling wild animals, right next to a Nature Reserve!

When the tourists came down from the mountain every evening, restaurant waiters would wait to entice tourists into their restaurants.

"You're *most* welcome to *our* restaurant. You will love our wild game."

"Game in our restaurant is so fresh we kill it to order!"

★

Mo said to Bat Ears: "Let's go in with those tourists! We can pretend we are part of their family."

"No, I can't," said Bat Ears. "Most of the waiters are from our village. They know me. You go in and I'll stand guard for you."

Mo swaggered in to the big restaurant as if it was something he did every day. It was brightly lit inside and really busy. There was only one unoccupied table in a corner near the kitchen. Mo pulled out a chair and sat down.

No one paid any attention to Mo. The waiters were all busy: some were taking dishes to tables, some showing the menu to diners, and some directing diners to the kitchen to decide on which wild animals they wanted to eat.

The people at the table next to Mo were being served. For each dish served, a waiter gave an introduction.

"This is a stewed pangolin, which is nutritious."

"This is a roasted civet cat, which is delicious."

Mo jumped up and went over to the table. He

pointed to the stewed pangolin. "This pangolin is a National Class II protected animal."

Then Mo pointed at the roasted civet cat and said: "This is civet cat. Civet cats carry a terrible virus—"

The guests looked sick. One of them took out a few notes from his pocket, threw them on the table and walked out of the restaurant.

Other guests, seeing people leave without eating their food, wondered what was happening. One by one, they put down their bowls and chopsticks, left notes on the table, and left the restaurant.

The game restaurant was soon empty.

"What's going on?" asked the boss of the restaurant. He ordered his waiters to stand in a row.

"Tell me why those people left?"

"There was a child making trouble."

The boss said: "I have been sitting here all this time. Why didn't *I* see a child making trouble?"

"No... Not making trouble, exactly. He said some things to the guests..."

"What things?"

"I'm scared to say..."

"I'm asking you to say!"

"The boy said, 'the pangolin is a National Class II

protected animal.' He said, 'civet cats carry a terrible virus'—"

The waiters shuffled their feet.

"So pangolins are National Class II protected animals, are they?" asked the waiters.

"Will *we* be infected with the virus carried by civet cats?"

"Nonsense!" said the boss. "The child is talking nonsense. Where is the child, anyway?"

But Mo was nowhere to be seen.

★

While the waiters were being questioned in that restaurant, Mo was sitting in *another* restaurant looking at a menu. A waitress stood beside him, telling him about the game they could cook.

"Our restaurant has game from the sky, game from the earth and game from the waters. What would you like to eat, young man?"

"Can I look at the animals, before I decide, please?" asked Mo sweetly.

The waitress took Mo to a small room next to the kitchen, where there were lots of cages with animals inside.

The waitress was very enthusiastic. She wanted to impress Mo.

"Let me introduce the game that flies in the sky to you first. This is white crane and that is pheasant."

The white crane's feathers were *pure* white and the pheasant's brightly-coloured. Mo could imagine them flying in the sky, freely and gracefully. Now they were being kept in cages, about to be food on the table.

"I'll make them fly in the sky again!" Mo promised.

"Now let me introduce game that runs on the earth. This is a pangolin; this is civet cat; this is—"

"Wait a minute." Mo interrupted the waitress, "That sounds like a baby crying. It's coming from outside."

"Oh, that's the giant salamander," explained the waitress. "Take no notice."

"A Giant salamander? You have a giant salamander?"

"Yes. We do!" The waitress opened the door, and Mo saw a tank of water. "Look!"

Mo went over and had a look. What a *big* giant salamander! It was trying to get out of the tank, and crying like a baby.

Giant salamanders are valuable and rare! thought Mo. He took out his small digital camera.

The waitress was alarmed. "What are you doing?"

"I've never seen a giant salamander. So I want to take a photo of it."

"You can't do that! It is *not* permitted!"

The waitress tried to snatch Mo's camera. But Mo dodged about, taking photos of the giant salamander. Then he went back inside to snap the white crane, and the other animals.

SETTING GIANT SALAMANDER FREE

"Grab his camera!" shouted the waitress.

The other waiters tried to catch Mo.

"Little Jumper! Little Jumper! Over here." Bat Ears had been standing outside on guard. Mo threw the digital camera to him. "Catch, Bat Ears!"

"Grab that boy!" shouted the waiters

Now the waiters all ran after Bat Ears so Mo returned to the small room and opened the cages with the white crane and the pheasant in.

"Fly! You're free now! "

The white crane, with its long thin legs, and the pheasant, flapping its wings, ran out of the cages, spread their wings and flew up to the starry night sky.

Then Mo opened all the cages in the room. Pangolins, civet cats and other animals scampered away, out of the back door and up the mountain.

Mo was about to escape himself when he heard the giant salamander crying.

"Wa! Wa! Wa"

Mo had forgotten to save the giant salamander!

He lifted the giant salamander from the tank and escaped from the back door.

Mo wanted to find Bat Ears, but he also wanted to set the giant salamander free. What was more important at this very moment, Bat Ears or the giant salamander? Mo decided that it was the giant salamander, because its life was in danger. No one would want to capture Bat Ears for their restaurant!

★

Mo needed to find a mountain stream so he could save the giant salamander. There were mountain

streams everywhere, but it was difficult to see them at night. Mo would have to listen hard.

Gurgle, gurgle, gurgle.

Mo couldn't see what the mountain stream looked like in darkness, but from its silvery sound, he could imagine it was full and fast-flowing. This was where the giant salamander belonged.

Mo carefully placed the giant salamander into the stream.

"Swim, giant salamander," he shouted. "Go, the farther, the better! Don't get caught again."

Now Mo had to get home without anyone from the restaurants seeing him. He didn't dare go back the same way.

Mo finally scrambled down a rough path. It wasn't long before he saw tiny spots of lamplight below – the village!

First of all, Mo went to Bat Ears' home to see if he had come back.

Bat Ears had been home for ages. He'd eaten three bowls of rice and gone straight to sleep.

Bang! Bang! Bang!

Mo knocked on the door.

"Who is it?" Bat Ears mum opened the door. "It's

you, Little Jumper! Bat Ears is asleep. You'd better come and play with him tomorrow!"

Mo was happy. Bat Ears was OK, so was the camera. He knew Bat Ears wouldn't have slept if he had lost Mo's camera. And best of all, *all* the animals from the restaurant were free!

HiDE AND SEEK

The old ginkgo tree was the biggest in the village. People said it was one thousand years old. Its leaves were bright green in summer, while in autumn they were golden. It was the children's favourite place to play games. Mo and Bat Ears and some other children were going to play there this afternoon. They were taking a rest from feeding monkeys and rescuing animals!

"What shall we play, Little Jumper?" asked the children.

"Let's play hide-and-seek with the big yellow dog."

Mo said, "The big yellow dog can sniff your clothes and get your scent. I'll blindfold the dog and give you ten minutes to hide. Then I'll send the dog to look for you."

The children stood in a row to let the big yellow dog sniff their clothes.

The big yellow dog sniffed very carefully, from the feet all the way up as far as her nose could reach.

"OK. Run as soon as I blindfold the big yellow dog," said Mo.

Mo put a strip of black cloth over the big yellow dog's eyes, and the children ran in all directions.

Ten minutes later, Mo took the black strip from the dog's eyes, and the big yellow dog started running right away, sniffing the ground as it went.

First it ran to a well, barking loudly.

"Woof woof! Woof woof! Woof woof!"

Mo bent over the mouth of the well. It didn't have any water in it, and there was Bat Ears sitting at the bottom.

"Come up, Bat Ears! We've found you!" shouted Mo.

"How did the big yellow dog find me so quickly?" Bat Ears moaned. "She must be very smart to sniff me out down such a deep well."

Mo said, "You're with me all day long, so she knows your smell, especially your pongy feet!" Mo helped Bat Ears out of the well.

Next, the big yellow dog ran to the big lotus pool. It was full of lotus flowers, with big leaves that lay on the surface of the water.

"Woof, woof! Woof, woof! Woof, woof!"

It was very quiet at the lotus pool, except for the dog's barking. The big yellow dog would not stop.

Someone *must* be hiding here.

The dog was about to dash into the water, but Mo stopped it. He shouted to the lotus pool, "Come out! The big yellow dog has found you."

Maidong swam over. He had hidden in the water and put a giant lotus leaf on his head!

"I thought the big yellow dog couldn't follow a smell in water."

Maidong climbed ashore, took off his wet trousers, then ran to a big rock where he'd hidden his clothes.

Now the big yellow dog ran off again. Mo, Bat Ears *and* Maidong followed it.

The big yellow dog ran towards Grandpa Hutu's cornfield.

Grandpa Hutu, who had just woken up, was singing a Chinese opera while drinking tea.

"Qiangqiang! Qiangqiang! Qiangqiang! Qiang!"

Seeing the big yellow dog, Grandpa Hutu put her into his song, "The big yellow dog is running like the wind, yi...ya...yi ..."

"Woof, woof! Woof, woof! Woof, woof!"

The big yellow dog rushed into Grandpa Hutu's shack and pulled Mizi out by his trousers.

The big yellow dog was now followed by Mo, Bat Ears, Maidong and Mizi. It barked again after a few steps.

"This is Mugua's house," Bat Ears said. "What kind of idiot hides in his own house?"

The gate of Mugua's home was locked tight.

The big yellow dog barked more loudly, rushing at the gate like a mad dog.

A head appeared over the wall. It was Mugua's mother.

"Hey, what are you up to?" she shouted.

"We're playing hide-and-seek. Please open the gate and let us in!"

"No!" said Mugua's mother, crossly. "Go away!"

Mo and the other boys thought it was very strange. No one in the village closed their gate in the daytime. Why wouldn't Mugua's mother let them in? And why did she look so cross?

THE SECRET OF
THE SHED

"Woof! Woof! Woof!"

The big yellow dog threw itself against the gate. But it stayed shut.

"Isn't Mugua at home?"

"He must be," said Mo. "If he wasn't at home, the big yellow dog wouldn't bark so much."

The big yellow dog kept on barking and looked as if it would not stop until the gate was open.

The gate opened and Mugua's mum came out.

"Why are you making such a racket?" she asked.

"We want to find Mugua," said Bat Ears.

"Well, he's not at home."

"He must be," argued Mo. "The big yellow dog has tracked his smell."

"I've just said that he is *not* at home," insisted Mugua's mother.

While Mugua's mum was answering Mo, the big yellow dog had leaped through the gate and into the house.

"Out! Out!" Mugua's Mum screamed, and went to chase the dog out.

"Woof! Woof! Woof!"

But the big yellow dog had found Mugua. She grabbed him by the seat of his trousers and dragged him out into the courtyard.

Mugua wore short trousers with an elastic waistband. The dog pulled them so much that the boys could see Mugua's bum. They all giggled.

The big yellow dog let the boy go, then turned around and ran towards Mugua's house again.

"Big yellow dog, come back!"

The big yellow dog paid no attention to Mo's order and threw itself against the door of the house.

"This is weird!" said Bat Ears. "Has the big yellow dog gone mad?"

"Mugua, is something hidden in your house?"

Mugua looked nervous.

Bat Ears whispered to Mo, "I bet they've got pangolins hidden in there."

Mo suddenly said, "Mugua, I *know* that you have pangolins hidden in your house."

"No, no, no, we haven't got any pangolins."

Mo was determined to find out the truth. The game of hide-and-seek was over, and all the children went away.

But Mo and Bat Ears didn't go home. They went to Grandpa Hutu's shack because they would be able to see Mugua's house from there.

After the children had left, Mugua didn't go straight into the house. He kept looking back to make sure that Mo and the other children had really gone. Then he unlocked the door with his key and slammed it shut as soon as he had entered.

 109

"There must be something wrong at Mugua's house," said Mo. "But we can't see clearly enough." Then he remembered something he had at Grandma and Grandpa's house.

Mo went home and came back with the telescope he'd brought with him for the holidays. He and Bat Ears got a little closer to Mugua's house. They hid behind some green trees, but Bat Ears also made two hats out of branches for both of them, as camouflage. Now no one would see them!

Mo looked through the telescope. He could see Mugua's house and the garden very clearly now.

Bat Ears was desperate to use the telescope. "Let me have a look! Let me have a look!" he whispered, eagerly.

"Be quiet, Bat Ears! I've seen something!"

In the middle of the garden, there was a little shed built of bricks. There were no windows, just a small door. An evil-looking man kept walking in and out and every time he walked in or out, he closed the door very carefully.

Mo gave the telescope to Bat Ears. Bat Ears was amazed at how much he could see through the telescope. "What's that shed? He's never let us play hide-and-seek in it."

Mo asked Bat Ears who the man walking in and out was. Bat Ears said that he was Mugua's dad.

"Oh! Now there's another man coming!"

Mo grabbed the telescope: a short, angry-looking man walked into the shed.

"Who's that?" asked Mo.

"I don't know," Bat Ears answered. "He doesn't live in our village."

After a while, the short man came back. He opened the door, and it was very bright inside. But this time, he forgot to shut it behind him.

Mo and Bat Ears took turns to use the telescope.

"Bat Ears, what do you think they're up to?"

"There must be something dodgy going on."

"No wonder the big yellow dog kept barking."

"I see it! I see it!" Bat Ears suddenly shouted.

Mo grabbed the telescope, but the door was closed when he looked through it.

"Bat Ears, what did you see?"

"They were bundling something black into the shed."

"What sort of something?"

"It looked like a big black bear."

"A big black *bear*?" Mo stood up. "Are you sure?"

Bat Ears nodded and then shook his head, "I think so... But I didn't see it very clearly."

"We need to call the police!"

MO TO THE RESCUE

Mo called the police from his mobile.

"Come quickly," he yelled. "We've found a captured black bear. It's being kept prisoner in a shed."

"Where are you calling from, young man? We'll get there as soon as possible."

"Wanglong Village. We'll wait for you under the dragon fountain in the village square."

They hung up and rushed to the village square. There was the flying dragon fountain right in the middle. No one could miss it when they got to the village.

Bat Ears sat on the back of the flying dragon, watching the road.

"They're coming! They're coming. Four cops riding fast motorbikes!"

Mo heard the roaring of engines coming nearer and nearer. Four motorbikes stopped right in front of them.

"Hop on and show us the way, boys!"

Mo jumped on to the first motorcycle, clasped the officer's waist, and guided them to the trees where they had spied on Mugua's house.

"Officer, first look through my telescope."

The officer looked through the telescope. He frowned. He gave the telescope back to Mo saying, "Boys, you stay here."

He took out his gun and shouted to the other police officers, "Ready for action!"

With guns in hands, the police officers stormed Mugua's house.

Shortly after, Mo and Bat Ears saw two sullen-looking, handcuffed men walking out of the yard with two of the officers.

One of the officers was using his mobile to ask the Black Bear Rescue Centre to send doctors. They said that they'd found a black bear in a cage, and that it was very poorly.

While they were waiting for the doctor, the police questioned Mugua's dad. He confessed that the black bear had only been a few months old when they had captured it. For eleven years, it had been kept in an iron cage in the shed, unable to see the sunshine.

Half an hour later, an ambulance arrived and a doctor and two nurses got out. The doctor was English and her name was Dr Lorraine. She had been in China for years and years and spoke Chinese very fluently.

"Where is the black bear?"

Mo jumped in front of Dr Lorraine, "I'll show you."

Dr Lorraine looked at the boy in a surprise. Why was there was a child with the cops?

One of the officers told Lorraine that it was the boy and his friend who had called them and told them about the captured bear.

"Oh, well done, young men!" Lorraine said, "Please show me the way!"

Mo took Dr Lorraine and the nurses to the front of the little shed. They opened the narrow door and out came a disgusting rotten smell.

When it saw the strangers enter, the black bear

 115

began to hit the cage furiously and roared desperately.

"Don't be afraid, baby!" Dr Lorraine smiled and walked towards the bear while making a calming gesture. "We're here to help you."

She said lots to comfort the bear and it slowly calmed down.

A rescue worker fed the bear with apples and pineapples cut into small chunks. The bear ate with great difficulty because its teeth had all rotted away.

While the black bear was busy eating fruit, Dr Lorraine took out a long syringe and injected the bear.

Twenty minutes later, the black bear fell into a deep sleep. The doctors opened the cage, moved the bear on to a gigantic stretcher and carried it out. Dr Lorraine began to examine the bear. It was covered in cuts and bruises.

"Look at these teeth," said Dr Lorraine. "They should be several centimetres long, but after years of biting the cage, they're all worn down."

"No wonder it has such smelly breath," said Bat Ears.

Mo asked Dr Lorraine why the bear had some many cuts and bruises.

"It must have got very bad tempered from not being able to see the sky or the sun. It probably banged against the bars a lot."

Dr Lorraine said she was going to take the black bear to the Black Bear Rescue Centre for further treatment before it woke up. She said goodbye to Mo and Bat Ears.

"You are brave and caring boys. I wish all children were as kind to animals as you two are."

Doctor Lorraine said that she had a present for the boys. She took two black velvet bears from the ambulance, and said, "These are special toys for people who help black bears."

Then the white ambulance drove off, carrying the big black bear to the Centre for treatment.

★

It was getting dark. Mo walked towards Grandpa and Grandma's house with his black velvet bear. On his way home, he felt sad – how could people be so cruel?

As Mo stepped into the garden of Grandpa and Grandma's house, he saw a familiar car in the yard.

It was his dad's car! Dad was here!

"Dad, why are *you* here?" asked Mo.

"Why am I here? I've come to take you back. You must be forgetting that school starts tomorrow. Time flies when you're having fun, doesn't it?"

School was about to start? Oh, no! The summer holidays were over. Yes, time did fly when you were having fun. In fact, it was gone in the twinkle of an eye.

READER'S NOTE

MO'S WORLD

Mo Shen Ma lives in a big city in China. Modern Chinese cities are very much like ours, so his life is not so different from your own: he goes to school, watches television and gets up to mischief – just like children all over the world!

There are *some* differences, though. Chinese writing is completely unlike our own. There is no alphabet, and words are not made up of letters – instead, each word is represented by a little drawing called a *character*. For us, learning to read is easy. There are only twenty-six letters that make up all our words! But in Chinese, every word has its own character. Even Simplified Chinese writing uses a core of 6,800 different characters. Each character has to be learned by heart, which means that it takes many years for a Chinese school student to learn to read fluently.

NAMES

Chinese personal names carry various meanings and the names in this book have definitely been chosen for a reason! Take Mo Shen, the hero of our tale. His name is made up of the word *Mo*, which means "good ideas" and *Shen*, which means "deep" or "profound". So you can see how much his name suits him, because Mo Shen is always coming up with great ideas! And then there's Grandpa Hutu. *Hutu* means absentminded – which we think you'll agree suits Grandpa Hutu pretty well!

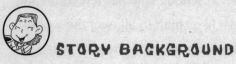

STORY BACKGROUND

In the book you've just read, Mo tries to make other people think about endangered species – especially the *pangolin*, which is a sort of scaly anteater found in China. As Mo explains to Bat Ears, pangolins are not protected because they are *rare* – actually there are quite a lot of them. The reason people are not allowed to hunt them is that they eat termites, and if pangolins were to disappear, the termites would quickly multiply and start to eat any wood they could find – including people's houses!

Chinese people take the idea of a plague of insects very seriously. That's because of something that happened there during a time called the Cultural Revolution, in the late 1960s. This was a period in which the leaders of the People's Republic of China tried to make huge changes to

Chinese society. One of their ideas was to get everyone in the country to kill as many sparrows as they could. They thought that this would stop the birds from eating seeds in the fields, which would mean that crops would be more successful and everyone would have more to eat. People all over China began to kill sparrows, using whatever weapons they could find.

Millions of birds died. So, now there were no sparrows to eat the seeds in the fields. And if there were more seeds, there must have been bigger crops and lots of food for everyone to eat, right?

Wrong. What the government didn't realise is that sparrows don't actually eat that many seeds. What they eat *most* of is locusts. But now there were no sparrows to keep the locust population down. Pretty soon, there was a major plague of locusts all over China. These locusts ate up all the seeds that the people thought they'd saved by killing the sparrows – and soon the crops started to fail. Many people died of starvation. And that's why, when Mo says that killing pangolins is a serious business, he really means it…